LOOKOUT
POINT

CHARITY

THE ILAS

LADYFACE

LABYRINTH

ILA VISTA

PARADISE
COVE

KNOTTY PINE

GENERAL STORE

Toys

CANDY

SCHOOL HOUSE

FIRESIDE

WANDERING
ROAD

Welcome to the
World of

W W ™

WILLOWBE WOODS
Campfire Stories

The Moon In My Room

Written by
Ila Wallen

Illustrated by
Robert Sauber

Willowbe Woods Campfire Stories
Created by
Bill Wallen & Ila Wallen

BENT WILLOW
PUBLISHING

BENT WILLOW
PUBLISHING

2260 Townsgate Road Suite #2
Westlake Village, CA 91361
(805) 381-1033
www.bentwillowpublishing.com

The Moon In My Room

Bill Wallen - Publisher & Art Director • Patrick Davidson - Editorial Director • Carolyn Wallen - Editor
Michael Wallen - Designer • Rich Conturo - Graphic Art Production

The Willowbe Woods Campfire Stories
Created by
Bill Wallen & Ila Wallen

Printed in the United States by Phoenix Color, Rockaway, N. J.
10 9 8 7 6 5 4 3 2

Publisher's Cataloging-in-Publication

Wallen, Ila
The moon in my room / by Ila Wallen;
illustrated by Robert Sauber – 1st ed.
p. cm. – (Willowbe Woods Campfire Stories ; 1)

SUMMARY: Will, a young bear, strongly suggests
that Papa Rango tell the assembled woodland creatures
about how he overcame his fear of the dark.

ISBN 0-9710627-0-6

1. Fear -- Juvenile fiction. 2. Problem solving --
Juvenile fiction. 3. Forest animals -- Juvenile fiction.
[1. Fear -- Fiction. 2. Problem solving -- Fiction.
3. Forest animals -- Fiction. 4. Stories in rhyme]
I. Sauber, Robert, ill. II. Title

PZ8.3.W175Mo2002   [E] - QB101-700614

To my parents:
For instilling in me the strength
to reach for my dreams and the creativity
to make them come true.
- Ila Wallen

To all of us who were afraid of the dark,
and came to see the light.
- Robert Sauber

Take my hand and follow me
To the enchanted woods of Willowbe.
Laughter and warmth surround the campfire
In Willowbe Woods, where stories inspire.

Papa Rango greets friends from far and near
With happy hugs and a welcoming cheer.
The Willowbeings gather together each night
For stories and songs that bring joy and delight.

Bent Willow remembers each tale that is told.
Within her leaves are stories new and old.
At Fireside, Papa Rango opens his storybook with care,
And asks, "Tonight whose story shall I share?"

"Read mine!" "No, mine!" "My story's the best!"
"Please pick mine from all the rest!"
From around the tree all the kids shout,
But only one voice clearly stands out.

It is Will's, the young bear, his voice booming with might,
"Please, Papa Rango, share my story tonight.

The one where I thought something was under my bed;
The one where I learned being scared was just in my head."

"What a wonderful choice," Rango says with delight.
"Here we go, let me start, Once upon a Willowbe Night . . ."

Will was alone in his room and the lights were out,
When he thought he heard something and let out a shout.

Shivering and shaking, he wouldn't peek under his bed,
So he had his penguin pal Fred take a look instead.

His room was too dark, and Will couldn't see.
He yelled, "DADDY, I need you! Come here to me."

Hⁱˢ dad, Billy, rushed in with a
THUD THUMP BOOM.
"What is it, Will? Is something in your room?"

He had a flashlight in his large grizzly bear paw.
"Tell me what's wrong, tell me what you saw."

"It's too dark in my room and
There's something under my bed.

Please make it go away,"
Will said with much dread.

So Billy looked everywhere
With his trusty flashlight,

To make sure everything
In Will's room looked
Just right.

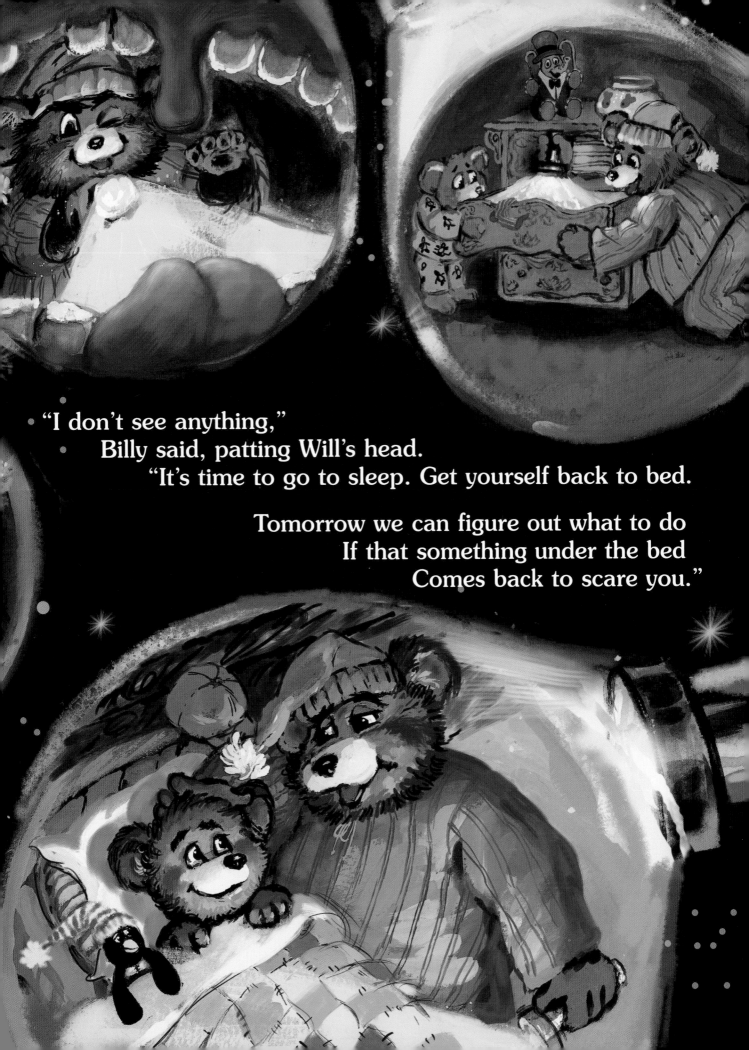

"I don't see anything,"
        Billy said, patting Will's head.
            "It's time to go to sleep. Get yourself back to bed.

                Tomorrow we can figure out what to do
                    If that something under the bed
                        Comes back to scare you."

The next morning, sleepy Will
Was cranky and groggy.
Staying awake all night had
Made his head feel foggy.

Then a thought came to him,
"My friends will know what to do.
Maybe something under their bed
Has been scaring them too."

Bandit the Raccoon was busy fishing at Thinker's Rock.
Will skipped over to him and took a seat on the dock.

"Bandit, help me get rid of the thing that I dread!
I'm afraid of the dark and there's something under my bed."

Bandit thought for a minute and snapped his fingers with glee.
"I'm not afraid of the dark, but bright lights sure bother me.

Maybe you could borrow the cool sunglasses I wear.
They might give that something under your bed a real scare."

"No, Bandit, I don't think your sunglasses will do.
They won't work for me,
Though they sure work for you.

I'm afraid of the dark and the
Something under my bed.

All your sunglasses will do
Is sit on top of my head."

Will went looking for Sophie the Fox
   And found her at the tree house singing with her jukebox.

Will called up to Sophie, "I need some advice from you.
   It'll just take a minute and you'll know what to do."

"I'm afraid of the dark and there's something under my bed.
I'd much rather keep the lights in my room on instead."

"The dark does not scare me," Sophie said, "but high places used to.
Then I got a trampoline and saw sights that were new.

Now I'm no longer afraid to climb high.
Borrow my trampoline and give it a try."

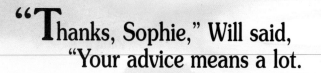

"Thanks, Sophie," Will said,
    "Your advice means a lot.

But your trampoline will not help me,
    It definitely will no-o-o-o-o-o-t!"

Will saw Flynn the Wolf eating lunch near Mystic Lake.
He had a jelly sandwich and yummy chocolate cake.
"Flynn, my friend, may I ask you a question?
I'm afraid of the dark. Do you have a suggestion?"

Flynn took a deep breath and let out a sigh,
"I'm too cool to be afraid of the dark, little guy.
But going under water is something I fear.
I feel better when I use my cool snorkel gear."

"You can borrow it if
    You think it will help you,
And if that doesn't work,
    There's always kung-fu."

Will laughed and giggled
    At the suggestions Flynn gave,
But he knew none would work
    And said good-bye with a wave.

Will walked back home,
　　His face dressed in a frown,
When Bunny the Rabbit
　　Tracked him down.

"I hear you need help,
　　That something scares you.
I want you to know
　　That I was scared of things too."

"Like wiggly worms, muckity muck, and mushy meals,
　　But loud noises are what really give me the squeals.

I think my fluffy ear muffs could be of some use.
　　They keep sounds out with feathers that come from a goose."

Bunny's suggestion
  Just didn't seem right,
So Will thanked his friend
  For help in his plight.

Then Bunny asked him something
  No one else had,
"Will, what makes you feel safe
  When you're feeling bad?"

Will scratched his head, then on his face beamed a smile.
"I know where I feel safe; I've known all the while.

In my room, oh yes, when the moon shines bright,
I need the moon in my room to make me feel right."

Will burst into his house like a whirling cyclone.
"Daddy, I figured out what will help me all on my own!
The idea in my head came just like a spark.
I know what will help me feel safe in the dark."

Will told his Daddy he wanted the moon as a light,
Then Billy suggested something that would work just as bright.
"A night light glows strong and it's something you keep,
A night light would work; it stays on while you sleep."

At the general store, Will found a perfect night light.
It was a great big moon that he knew would be just right.

Later that evening, Will never made a peep.
With the moon in his room, he fell fast asleep.

"And that's how Will's fear of the dark went away,"
Papa Rango says, closing his book for the day.

"Come back tomorrow night
At the same time and same place

For another Willowbe Story
That will put a smile on your face."

There are yawns and big hugs
Under the night sky so clear.

Papa Rango bids "Good Night"
To his friends who are dear.

Laughter and warmth
Surround the campfire,

In Willowbe Woods,
Where stories inspire.

The End

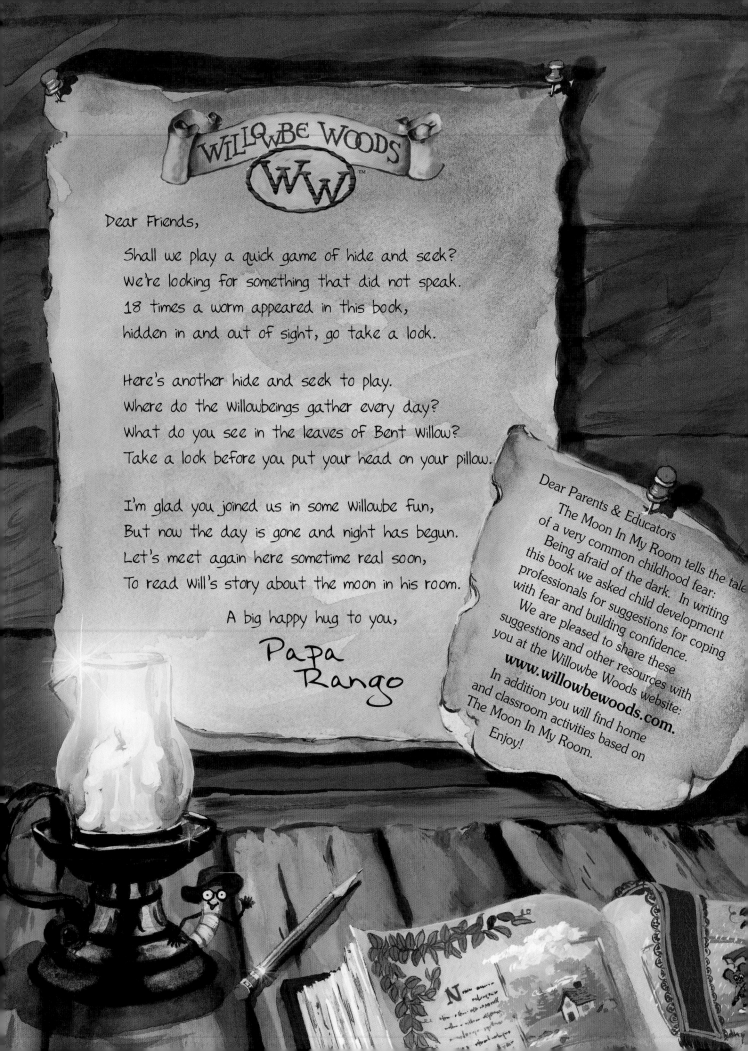

WILLOWBE WOODS
WW™

Dear Friends,

Shall we play a quick game of hide and seek?
We're looking for something that did not speak.
18 times a worm appeared in this book,
hidden in and out of sight, go take a look.

Here's another hide and seek to play.
Where do the Willowbeings gather every day?
What do you see in the leaves of Bent Willow?
Take a look before you put your head on your pillow.

I'm glad you joined us in some Willowbe fun,
But now the day is gone and night has begun.
Let's meet again here sometime real soon,
To read Will's story about the moon in his room.

A big happy hug to you,

Papa Rango

Dear Parents & Educators
    The Moon In My Room tells the tale
of a very common childhood fear.
    Being afraid of the dark. In writing
this book we asked child development
professionals for suggestions for coping
with fear and building confidence.
    We are pleased to share these
suggestions and other resources with
you at the Willowbe Woods website:
www.willowbewoods.com.
    In addition you will find home
and classroom activities based on
The Moon In My Room.
    Enjoy!